Evie's
Mad Hair Day

Shane McG

templar publishing

I'm Evie.

When I wake up in the morning I always have a really big stretch.

To Evie, because you're so clever – S.M.

A TEMPLAR BOOK

First published in the UK in 2005 by Templar Publishing,

an imprint of The Templar Company plc,

Pippbrook Mill, London Road, Dorking, Surrey, RH4 1JE, UK

www.templarco.co.uk

Copyright © 2005 by Shane McG

First edition

ISBN 1-84011-862-8

Printed in China

It takes me less than four minutes to get dressed...

and seven minutes to eat my cereal for breakfast,
                depending on how much I spill on the table...

    and on the floor...

    and in my shoe (don't ask).

Then there's three more minutes cleaning my teeth.

Up, down, up, down...
    YAWN. Boring!

By the time I've finished all that, I've no time to brush my hair.

So I'm having a Mad Hair Day!

Who cares?

I have places to go, things to do.

And brushing my hair is **not** one of them.

I'm too busy...

sitting
in
this
old
cardboard
box.

Well, obviously it's not **really** a box.

It's a very sleek and fast red sports car...

Perfect for a spot of shopping!

So what if I have **Mad Hair**?

I'm much too busy riding on this very long broom.

(It's easier said than done, you know.)

When I say broom I don't really **mean** broom. (I'm not silly.)

I mean a big, brown, galloping horse.

I ride across vast green fields and shout 'YIPPEE!'

(And try not to scare the cows.)

Mad hair, **who cares?**

I don't. Oh no!

I'm far too busy jumping in the air!

And boy, do I jump high!

So high, I feel like I'm in space.
That's pretty high, let me tell you.

But exciting too.

Have you ever been in space?

It's pretty crowded
up there!

Mad hair,
who cares?

I'm way too busy at the moment.

Somebody has to keep Nat the Cat, and the toys entertained.

Which is why **I have to BANG** on this empty saucepan.

Very Loudly!

See, it's working already.

I absolutely
definitely
won't ever
in a million
years

brush my mad hair.

I'm far too busy   singing in this mirror.

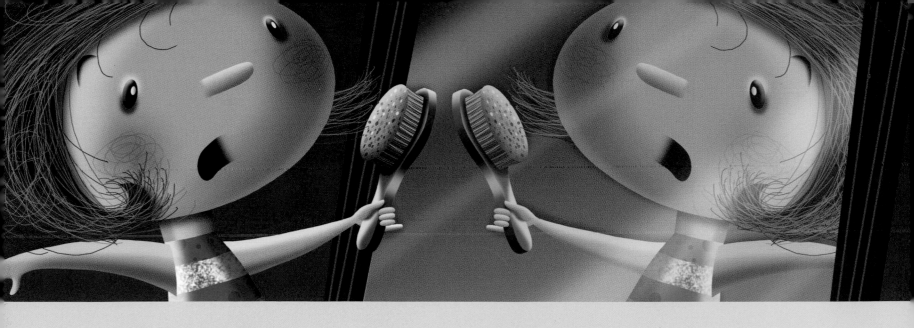

Huh?

Oh dear...   well, maybe just a little brush.

Now, I'm ready to meet my friends James, Phoebe and Calem.

We're off to do some **serious playing**.